A Mis

"Can we take a peek at your doll?" Ellen asked Caroline.

"We promise not to touch it," Elizabeth added.

"Well, all right," Caroline said. "Just a peek. She's my most beautiful doll."

Jessica held her breath while Caroline snapped open the fasteners of the small travel case. Very slowly, she raised the lid. "She's under here," Caroline explained. She lifted out white tissue paper and gasped.

The case was empty!

"My doll!" Caroline cried. "Somebody took my doll!"

Bantam Skylark Books in the SWEET VALLEY KIDS series

SWEET VALLEY KIDS

CAROLINE'S MYSTERY DOLLS

Written by
Molly Mia Stewart

Created by
FRANCINE PASCAL

Illustrated by
Ying-Hwa Hu

A BANTAM SKYLARK BOOK⁶
NEW YORK · TORONTO · LONDON · SYDNEY · AUCKLAND

RL 2, 005–008

CAROLINE'S MYSTERY DOLLS
A Bantam Skylark Book / April 1991

Sweet Valley High® and Sweet Valley Kids are trademarks of
Francine Pascal

Conceived by Francine Pascal

Produced by Daniel Weiss Associates, Inc.
33 West 17th Street
New York, NY 10011

Cover art by Susan Tang

Skylark Books is a registered trademark of Bantam Books, a division of
Bantam Doubleday Dell Publishing Group, Inc. Registered in U.S. Patent
and Trademark Office and elsewhere.

ISBN 0-553-15870-8

Published simultaneously in the United States and Canada

Bantam Books are published by Bantam Books, a division of Bantam Double-
day Dell Publishing Group, Inc. Its trademark, consisting of the words "Ban-
tam Books" and the portrayal of a rooster, is Registered in U.S. Patent and
Trademark Office and in other countries. Marca Registrada. Bantam Books,
666 Fifth Avenue, New York, New York 10103.

PRINTED IN THE UNITED STATES OF AMERICA

OPM   14 13 12 11 10 9 8 7 6 5

To Sasha Grodzin

CHAPTER 1

Jessica's Challenge

Elizabeth Wakefield and her twin sister, Jessica, were on their way to the bus stop one school morning. Elizabeth was walking with her books balanced on her head. "See if you can walk this way," she said to Jessica.

"Of course I can," Jessica answered quickly. She took three steps down the sidewalk and her schoolbooks fell. "It's not as easy as it looks," she said, laughing.

Elizabeth and Jessica were identical twins. They both had blue-green eyes and long blond hair with bangs. When they dressed in matching outfits, it was difficult to tell them apart. Sometimes even their best friends had to check their name bracelets.

The best way to tell one twin from the other was to talk to each one. Elizabeth usually talked about the books she was reading or animals or her homework. She was always eager to say something nice to a friend, too. Jessica always had a secret to share or a joke to tell. She only liked school because it was where she saw her friends.

Even though Jessica and Elizabeth looked exactly alike on the outside, they were quite different on the inside. But no matter how different they were, they were best friends. They shared a room, they shared clothes, and they each had a special way of knowing what the other twin was thinking or feeling.

"First one to the bus stop is a rotten string bean," Jessica called suddenly.

The two girls started running. Elizabeth won by a second.

"Hi, Elizabeth. Hi, Jessica," Caroline Pearce said as they arrived at the bus stop. Caroline was in Mrs. Otis's second grade class with the twins.

Elizabeth smiled. "Hi, Caroline."

Jessica looked at Caroline and frowned. No one in class liked Caroline very much. She was always trying to be the teacher's pet. Recently she had been bragging about having a collection of porcelain dolls.

"Caroline," Jessica began, "I've been thinking about your porcelain dolls. How come you've never told us about them before?" she said. "We have Show and Tell all the time. Why haven't you brought your dolls in?"

"I just haven't, that's all," Caroline said.

"I'll bet you made it all up," Jessica answered.

Caroline's face turned pink. "I did not!"

3

"Then let me see them." Jessica smiled. "Why don't you invite me over after school?"

"Jessica!" Elizabeth whispered. "That's mean."

"You can't come over," Caroline said quickly. "My parents have guests, so I can't play indoors."

Jessica crossed her arms. "We don't have to play. I just want to see your dolls."

Charlie Cashman was standing nearby. "Ooooh! Can I see your dolls, too?" he asked in a high voice. He was in their class, too, and he loved to tease everyone. He especially loved to tease Caroline, because she always became upset when he did.

"You be quiet, Charlie," Caroline said. "Or else I'm telling on you."

Charlie pretended to be scared. "Oh,

no!" he said. Then he laughed and walked away.

"Caroline?" Jessica said again. "Can I come over after school?"

"But—" Caroline began. Then she stopped and pointed down the street. "Here comes the bus."

Everyone began pushing and shoving to get their place in line. Elizabeth tugged on Jessica's sleeve.

"How come you're bothering Caroline?" she asked.

"I'm not bothering her," Jessica said. "I just want to see her doll collection. I want to make sure she really has one."

Elizabeth looked over at Caroline, who was first in line. She could tell that Caroline was upset about Jessica's questions.

"I think you should be nicer to her," Elizabeth said in a quiet voice. She knew there was nothing she could do, though, because when her twin sister wanted to do something, nothing stood in her way.

CHAPTER 2

Show and Tell

Jessica put her books on her desk and walked over to talk to Lila Fowler who was standing by the windows. Lila was Jessica's best friend after Elizabeth. "I'm going to see Caroline's dolls this afternoon," Jessica said.

"She's a show-off," Lila said. "I've seen lots of dolls that I know are prettier than hers."

"Have you ever seen Caroline's dolls?" Jessica asked.

"No," said Lila.

"Then how do you know she has *any*

dolls?" Jessica said. "How do you know she's not making it all up?"

Lila's eyes widened. "Do you think she is?"

Jessica smiled. "Let's go find out."

Caroline was using the pencil sharpener at the back of the classroom. She looked up when Jessica and Lila walked over to her.

"Hi, Caroline," Lila said sweetly. "Jessica says you're going to show her your dolls. What are they like?"

"They're very delicate," Caroline said. "They each have a different, beautiful dress."

"I'll bet you keep them in a special place," Jessica said.

Caroline nodded. Ellen Riteman and Amy Sutton came over, too, so Caroline talked loud enough for them to hear. "My father built a special shelf in my room for all my dolls."

"I have a special shelf where I keep my stuffed animals," Amy said. "They hardly ever stay up there, though, since I play with them all the time."

"You can't play with porcelain dolls," Caroline said. "They break too easily."

"Why don't you bring your dolls to school?" Jessica suggested.

"What are you talking about?" Todd Wilkins asked as he walked up.

"Our special collections," Amy said.

"I've got a collection of baseball cards," Todd said. "I have sixty in all, and some are even autographed."

Others came over to join the conversation. "Eva has a collection of funny magnets," Ellen said. "And I love postcards of swans."

"I have the coolest marbles," Charlie said proudly.

There was such a large crowd around the pencil sharpener that Mrs. Otis walked to the back of the room. "What's going on?" the teacher asked.

"We're talking about all the things we like to collect," Jessica explained. "Caroline has the best collection of all. She has porcelain dolls."

"I love porcelain dolls," Mrs. Otis said with a big smile. "They're so lovely."

Then Mrs. Otis asked, "How many of you have collections?" When almost all the boys and girls raised their hands, she smiled. "Then let's have a special day. I want you all to bring in your collections to share with the class. Tomorrow will be an extra long Show and Tell."

"That means we'll get to see Caroline's dolls," Lila said.

"But—" Caroline began. Her face turned pink.

"Take your seats, everyone," Mrs. Otis said. "I want to announce this to the rest of the class."

Jessica hurried to her desk and sat down. Elizabeth sat in the seat next to her. "Now we'll get to see if Caroline is telling the truth," Jessica whispered while Mrs. Otis made her announcement. She was so pleased about the way things had turned out that she couldn't stop smiling.

"What are you going to bring in for *your* collection?" Elizabeth asked her.

Jessica's mouth dropped open. She hadn't thought about that, and she suddenly realized that she didn't have a collection—of anything! "I'm–I'm not sure," she said.

"Me, neither," Elizabeth said. "But I'll think of something."

Jessica wasn't so sure about her good mood anymore. Her plan to see Caroline's dolls had worked. But now she had to figure out a collection of her own to show.

CHAPTER 3

Two or More

Elizabeth watched the jumprope go around and around. She counted to three and jumped in with Jessica. Lila and Eva were turning the rope, while Amy and Ellen were watching.

"Do you have a collection, Lila?" Eva asked.

"Yes," Lila said, smiling mysteriously. "But I'm not telling. It's going to be a surprise."

"What kind of surprise?" Jessica wanted to know. "I never saw any special collection at your house."

"That's because I keep it in a secret drawer," Lila said in her know-it-all way.

Elizabeth concentrated on jumping, but she could tell that her sister was worried. Jessica was always talking about all the nice things Lila had. In Elizabeth's opinion, Lila was spoiled, but that didn't make Jessica feel any better.

"Uh-oh," Ellen said. "Here comes Caroline."

"She always tries to barge in," Lila said.

"She probably wants to brag about her dolls some more," Amy said. "Who even cares about dolls?"

Elizabeth agreed with Amy. The two of them preferred to play outdoor games. Besides, Elizabeth preferred to cuddle *real* babies, such as their new next door neighbor, Jenny DeVito. She watched as Caroline sat down on a bench and looked at the ground.

Elizabeth could tell that Caroline was sad about something.

"I'm jumping out," she said to Amy. "You can jump in."

Elizabeth skipped out and walked over to Caroline. "Hi," she said, sitting down beside her on the bench.

"Hi," Caroline mumbled.

"Is something wrong?" Elizabeth asked.

Caroline shrugged. "I never wanted to bring my porcelain dolls in," she said. "But now I have to."

"But if they're so pretty, why don't you want everyone to see them?" Elizabeth asked.

"They could get broken," Caroline said quietly.

"They won't," Elizabeth said with a smile. "Don't worry. We'll all be very careful."

"Maybe." Caroline seemed to cheer up. She

looked at Elizabeth and smiled. "I saw a book about a unicorn on your desk. Can I read it when you're done?"

Caroline liked to borrow things, but she didn't always return them. "OK," Elizabeth said slowly. She knew it wasn't very nice not to want to lend Caroline the book. But she hurried back to her friends before Caroline asked to borrow anything else.

When they got home from school, Elizabeth and Jessica told their mother about Show and Tell.

"What collections are you going to bring in?" Mrs. Wakefield asked.

Elizabeth had already been thinking about it. "I'm going to show all my books about animals," she announced.

"Good idea," their mother said. "Your books make a lovely collection."

"What can I take?" Jessica asked. "I don't have a lot of anything special."

"A collection can be just a few things, you know," Mrs. Wakefield said encouragingly. "You probably have more collections than you realize."

Jessica shook her head. "I can't think of anything."

"Let's go look," their mother said. She held a hand out to each girl, and they all climbed the stairs together.

"I'll get all my books out," Elizabeth said, going to the bookcase in their bedroom.

Jessica looked around the room. She walked over to her dresser and pulled the hair ribbon out of her ponytail. There were

ribbons and headbands and barrettes piled on the dresser top.

"Look!" Jessica said. She scooped up the pile and brought it to her bed. "I can bring my hair things."

"That would be great," Mrs. Wakefield said.

"Yes," Elizabeth agreed. "I bet it'll be one of the biggest collections."

Jessica didn't seem so sure. "What about Lila?" she said, looking at her sister. "She's going to have something really, really good."

"Did Lila tell you what her collection was?" Mrs. Wakefield asked.

"No. But I don't want mine to look dumb," Jessica said.

"It won't," Elizabeth assured her. "Maybe you could even wear all of the ribbons at the same time."

"Ha, ha," Jessica said.

"Isn't this the headband you got for me?" Elizabeth asked as she picked up a light blue velvet headband with a bow on it.

Jessica nodded. Both girls remembered their seventh birthday party. Elizabeth had gotten Jessica a racecar, and Jessica had gotten Elizabeth a blue headband. But when they opened up their gifts, they quickly decided to switch. Each girl ended up keeping the present she had chosen for the other— the present each really wanted for herself.

"I'll take my racecars, too," Elizabeth said. "I have three of those, so that's a collection."

"I can't wait," Jessica said. "Between the two of us, we have a whole collection of collections!"

CHAPTER 4

Collections, Collections, Collections

The next morning Jessica was the first to get off the school bus. She couldn't wait to see Caroline's dolls. She rushed into the classroom and stopped in front of Caroline's desk. "Where are they?" she said.

Caroline was sitting up very straight in her chair. A small travel case covered with stickers and decals from different countries was on the floor under her desk. "I'm not showing you anything until it's time," she said.

"They're in there?" Jessica asked. Her eyes widened as she looked at the small case. "They must be tiny."

Caroline looked angry. "There's only one doll in there."

"No fair," Jessica said. She walked over to Lila, who was in the back of the room. "She only brought one doll," Jessica said. "That's not a collection."

Lila looked over at Caroline. "I hope Mrs. Otis calls on her first."

"Me, too," Jessica agreed.

But they had to wait until the end of the day for Mrs. Otis to announce that it was time to start showing the collections. "Who would like to go first?" she asked.

"Me, me!" Andy Franklin held up his hand in the front row. "Can I be first?"

Jessica was disappointed. Caroline hadn't even raised her hand.

"I brought my stamp collection," Andy explained. He put two large leather albums on Mrs. Otis's desk. "I started collecting stamps when I was five," he said.

Everyone left their seats and crowded around to see Andy's stamps. He pointed to each one and told the class where it came from.

"That one's from Jamaica!" Eva said happily as Andy pointed to a colorful stamp. She had moved to Sweet Valley from Jamaica, an island in the West Indies.

"My other international stamps are from France, China, and Canada," Andy said proudly.

Jessica began to feel worried. Andy's collection was much more interesting and

grown-up than hers, she decided. She started to think that people would laugh at her for bringing in barrettes and bows.

"That's an extremely interesting collection, Andy," Mrs. Otis said when he was finished. "I'll try to remember to give you all the unusual stamps that are on the envelopes I receive." She looked around. "Who would like to go next?"

"Me," Eva said. When Mrs. Otis nodded, Eva ran to her desk and got the shoebox that was on top. "I need to find something made out of metal," she said.

"The door is metal," Todd Wilkins called out.

Eva took her shoebox over to the door and began to stick tiny objects onto it. "This is my magnet collection," she explained. She had magnets that looked like cookies, hot dogs, and candy. There were magnets that looked like different kinds of animals, as well as magnets shaped like hearts, flowers, and stars. Eva had so many magnets that they covered most of the door.

"Those are really neat," Elizabeth said. "I want to start collecting magnets, too."

"I keep them all on our refrigerator," Eva explained.

Jessica looked at the paper bag on her desk. Inside were all her barrettes, ribbons, and headbands. Her collection seemed silly to her now. She crossed her fingers and hoped she wouldn't be called on.

Todd volunteered to be next. He showed his baseball cards. Then Elizabeth showed her books and her cars, Ken showed his stickers, and Sandra Ferris showed her six-foot-long gum-wrapper chain. Jessica kept glancing at the clock. She hoped the bell would ring.

Finally, when there was only a minute left, Mrs. Otis said, "I think we have time for one more collection." She looked at Jessica. "How about—"

RIIIING!

"Oh, dear. We'll have to finish up tomorrow," Mrs. Otis said.

While everyone gathered their books and left the classroom, Jessica walked over to Caroline's desk. "How come you didn't raise your hand?" she asked.

"I just didn't, that's all," Caroline said, putting the travel case on her desk.

Lila, Ellen, and Elizabeth came over. "Can't we just take a peek?" Ellen asked.

"We promise not to touch the doll," Elizabeth added.

Jessica nodded. "We just want to see her once."

"Well, all right," Caroline said. "Just a peek. She's my most beautiful doll."

Jessica held her breath while Caroline snapped open the fasteners. Very slowly, she raised the lid. There was white tissue paper inside.

"She's under here," Caroline explained. She lifted out the paper and gasped.

The case was empty!

"My doll!" Caroline cried. "Somebody took my doll!"

Jessica gulped. Who would have taken her doll? She glanced at Lila, and Lila looked as surprised as she did.

"Mrs. Otis!" Caroline cried, running to the teacher's desk. "Somebody stole my doll!"

"Maybe Charlie and Jerry hid it," Elizabeth said. "They're always playing jokes."

"They already left," Ellen pointed out. "We'll have to wait until tomorrow."

"We'll get to the bottom of this tomorrow," Mrs. Otis said. "I know how upset you are, Caroline. Whoever took the doll will give it back tomorrow. I'm sure of it."

"But it was m-m-my favorite doll!" Caroline sobbed.

"You have other dolls," Lila said.

That made Caroline cry harder.

Jessica looked at the empty case. *How could someone have taken Caroline's doll,* she wondered. *Or was there ever a doll in there in the first place?* One thing she did know was that Caroline's collection was becoming more mysterious every day.

CHAPTER 5

Caroline's Big Secret

Elizabeth unpacked her bookbag when she got home from school and put all her books back on the shelf. Then she remembered that Caroline wanted to borrow her book about the unicorn. She ran downstairs.

"Mom?" she called.

Mrs. Wakefield was reading the newspaper in the den. "Yes?" she asked.

"I told Caroline she could borrow this book from me," Elizabeth said. "Can I go over and give it to her?"

"Yes. But come right back home," her mother said.

Caroline lived only two houses away, so Elizabeth was allowed to walk there alone.

Mrs. Pearce answered the door when Elizabeth rang the bell.

"Hello, Mrs. Pearce," Elizabeth said. "Caroline wanted to borrow this book, so I brought it over."

"How thoughtful of you," Mrs. Pearce said. "Go right on to her room It's the second door on the left."

"I remember. Thank you." Elizabeth smiled and walked into the house. She had been there before and walked down the hall to Caroline's room. "Hi, Caroline!" she called. She knocked on the door softly.

Caroline opened the door and looked very

surprised. "What are you doing here?" she said.

"I brought you the book you wanted to read," Elizabeth said. She walked in and looked around the room. She didn't see a single porcelain doll anywhere. "Where are your dolls? she asked. "Didn't you say they were on a special shelf in your bedroom?"

Caroline's face turned bright red. "Ummm . . ." she stammered. Then she looked at Elizabeth and burst into tears.

"Don't tell anyone!" she said. "Please don't tell!"

Elizabeth felt angry and sad at the same time. Caroline had told a big lie. She didn't have a doll collection.

"But why did you make something up that you knew people would find out wasn't true?" Elizabeth asked.

Caroline sat on her bed. "I only have one doll, and I thought everybody would like me better if I had more," she said softly. "Now they'll just hate me because I'm a liar."

"But . . ." Elizabeth bit her lip. She couldn't think of anything to say.

"And now I don't even have one doll!" Caroline sobbed. "It was really special, too. It was very old."

Elizabeth wished she had never come over and found out Caroline's secret. It was sad that Caroline wanted everyone to like her so much that she would tell such a big lie.

"You won't tell anyone, will you?" Caroline asked. She wiped her eyes and looked at Elizabeth nervously.

"No, I won't," Elizabeth said. "But you shouldn't have bragged about something that wasn't true."

"I know," Caroline said. "I don't know what to do."

Elizabeth felt terrible. She knew she was not always as nice to Caroline as she was to everyone else. Now she realized that Caroline needed a friend.

"I'll help you tell the truth," Elizabeth said.

"I–I can't now," Caroline said, her voice shaking. "I just can't."

CHAPTER 6

Jessica's Collection

Jessica flopped onto her bed and stared at the ceiling. "This is dumb," she said out loud.

Spread all around her on the bed was her collection of barrettes, headbands, ribbons, and bows. After seeing the other things that her classmates had brought in, she was sure hers would look silly.

"What a dumb idea," she said.

Her older brother, Steven, looked in as he went down the hallway. "All your ideas are dumb," he teased.

"Go away," Jessica grumbled. There was a strange smell in the air, and she sniffed. "What's that smell?"

"It's part of my experiment for the fourth-grade science fair," Steven answered. "I'd explain it, but you wouldn't understand."

Steven walked down the hall to his room. Being in fourth grade made him feel much older than Jessica and Elizabeth. He really liked his two younger sisters, but he usually teased them. He liked inventing things and playing with his chemistry set.

Jessica was still thinking about her collection when Elizabeth walked in. "You have to help me, Liz," she said, sliding off the bed.

Elizabeth didn't answer right away. She just sat down at her desk.

"Where did you go?" Jessica asked. "I was looking for you."

"I took a book over to Caroline's house," Elizabeth answered.

Jessica's eyes lit up. "Did you get to see her dolls?" she asked.

Elizabeth looked out the window. "No," she said. She wished she could change the subject. "What did you need help with?"

"My collection," Jessica said. She swept her arms across her bed and gathered up all her barrettes and ribbons. "I'm not taking this stuff. It's too dumb."

"Then what are you going to take?" Elizabeth asked her. She picked up a pink ribbon with the name "Jessica" printed on it in blue letters.

"I don't know," Jessica said. She looked at

a white plastic barrette that spelled out "Jessica" in script. "I don't have anything else that's a collection."

"Yes you do," Elizabeth said with a big smile.

"Tell me what it is!" Jessica said. She looked around the room, but she couldn't figure out what her sister's idea was.

"Look." Elizabeth held out the ribbon and pointed to the barrette near Jessica. "You have a Jessica collection."

Suddenly, Jessica ran to her dresser and pulled open a drawer. Inside was a T-shirt with her name written across the front. Then she opened the closet and took out her sneakers. The shoelaces had "Jessica" printed on them.

"The license plate on my bike has 'Jessica' on it, and so do the paper lunch bags that

44

Grandma Wakefield gave me," Jessica said happily. "And I have some stickers with my name—"

"And your name bracelet," Elizabeth added. "I'll bet you'll have the only Jessica collection in the whole class, too."

Jessica smiled. "That's because I'm the only Jessica in the class." She looked around the room. "What else do I have with my name on it?"

"Your toothbrush says 'Jessica's Toothbrush' on it," Elizabeth reminded her.

"And this wooden puzzle," Jessica said. She rushed around the bedroom gathering her things. When she had them all together, she could see that it made a very large collection. "Do you think this is good enough?" she asked.

"Yes!" Elizabeth said.

Jessica didn't say anything for a moment. "I don't know if it'll be as good as Lila's, though. Lila will act really stuck-up if she has the best collection."

"She acts stuck-up anyway," Elizabeth teased.

"That's true. If Caroline brings the rest of her dolls in, her collection will be much better than anything Lila has," Jessica said cheerfully.

Elizabeth didn't answer. She just stared at the "Jessica" barrettes.

Jessica was too busy to notice that Elizabeth suddenly looked sad. She began putting her collection into a large paper bag. She couldn't wait to get to school the next day.

CHAPTER 7

Lost and Found

At the bus stop the next morning, the first two people the twins saw were Caroline and Charlie.

"You took my doll, Charlie Cashman!" Caroline was saying to him angrily. "Give it back."

"I don't have your dumb doll," Charlie said. He held out his hands and tried to look innocent. "See?"

"I know you took it," Caroline said. She sounded like she was going to start to cry.

Elizabeth wished she could find Caroline's

doll for her. She knew it was the only one Caroline had. Before Caroline and Charlie could argue any more, the bus pulled up and everyone got on.

"I'll bet Charlie *did* take it," Jessica whispered to Elizabeth when they found empty seats. "He's going to be in big trouble with Mrs. Otis."

Elizabeth thought her sister was right. As soon as they got to class, Mrs. Otis asked Charlie to come to her desk. Jerry McAllister was already there. His face was red.

"Now, boys," the teacher said in a very serious voice. "I don't want to accuse you unfairly, but I have to ask you. Did you take Caroline's doll yesterday? Did you hide it?"

Caroline stood behind Mrs. Otis and stared at the two boys. Jerry and Charlie

both looked at the floor. Elizabeth saw Jerry look at Charlie and make a face.

"We hid it," Jerry finally mumbled.

"I was right," Caroline said. "I knew it!"

Mrs. Otis put her finger to her lips to tell Caroline to be quiet. "Now boys, will you tell me where Caroline's doll is? The doll is very delicate and we don't want it to get damaged."

"It's in the trash can," Charlie said.

"The one in the back of the room," Jerry added, leading the way. He walked to the metal can and looked inside. "It's right—"

He became silent. Everyone turned around in their seats and stared at him.

"Jerry?" Mrs. Otis said.

Caroline's eyes widened. "It isn't there!" she cried, running to the can. "It's empty! My doll got thrown away!" Caroline began to cry.

Everyone in the class was quiet.

"We didn't mean for it to get thrown away," Charlie said.

"You're going to get into *so* much trouble," Jessica told him with a grin. Everyone in class was now out of their seats and standing by the trash can.

"Caroline, don't cry," Mrs. Otis said. She put her arm around Caroline's shoulder. "Why don't you go ask the custodian if he found the doll? I'm sure he wouldn't have thrown it away."

"I'll go with her," Elizabeth offered.

The teacher smiled. "That's nice of you, Elizabeth. Come on, Caroline. You and Elizabeth go find Jim. I'm sure he has your doll."

Elizabeth and Caroline walked down the hall. "I'll never see her again," Caroline said, between sobs.

"I'll bet Jim has her," Elizabeth said.

The two girls came to the janitor's office and knocked on the door. Caroline was still crying, so Elizabeth spoke up when Jim came to the door. "Did you find a porcelain doll yesterday?" she asked him. "It was in the trash can in Mrs. Otis's room."

Jim looked at Caroline's sad face and gave her a big, warm smile. "I sure did," he said. "I was just on my way to your classroom. Come on in."

"Oh!" Caroline gasped as she ran into the room. Sitting on a shelf was a beautiful doll with wavy red hair and a long, frilly blue dress. Caroline reached for the doll and hugged it tight. "Angelina!"

"You two run on back to class now," Jim said in a friendly voice.

"Thank you," Elizabeth said.

"Yes, thank you," Caroline said happily.

As they walked back down the hall, Elizabeth looked at Caroline's doll. "She really is beautiful," she said.

"I know," Caroline whispered.

"Are you going to tell everyone the truth?" Elizabeth asked.

Caroline hugged her doll again. "I have to," she said.

CHAPTER 8

Caroline's Collection

"Wow!" Jessica said, when she saw Caroline's doll. Almost everyone in the room crowded around Caroline—even Amy, who didn't like dolls.

"Oh, can I hold her?" Eva asked.

"Can I?" Lila asked.

"You got her back safe and sound, I see," Mrs. Otis said with a happy smile. "Why don't you tell us about her right now, Caroline?"

Jessica wanted a chance to hold the doll more than anything. It was even more beautiful than she had imagined. But Mrs. Otis was telling everyone to go sit down again.

"OK," Caroline said. She walked to the front of the room. She was smiling as she held her doll tight. "This is Angelina," she began.

A few of the boys pretended to cough, but Mrs. Otis said "Sshh!" loudly. "Listen carefully, everyone," she said.

"Her face and arms are made of porcelain," Caroline said. "That's like china dishes, so she could break really, really easily. And she was painted by an artist."

Jessica could see that Angelina had blue eyes, the same color as her dress, and a pink heart-shaped mouth.

"Angelina first belonged to my grandmother's grandmother who was born in Germany a long time ago," Caroline went on.

"That's where Angelina was made. When my great grandmother came to America on a boat, she brought Angelina with her in that tiny suitcase." She pointed to the small brown case covered with stickers that sat on her desk.

"It looks like Angelina has traveled all over the world," Mrs. Otis said, looking at the stickers that said "Paris," "London," and "Brussels."

"She has," Caroline said proudly. "And each time there was a new baby girl in the family, Angelina was given to her. If there wasn't a girl, Angelina was given to the granddaughter. Our family kept moving across the country with the pioneers. My grandmother was born in Colorado. Then my father moved to California, and that's when my grandmother gave Angelina to me."

Caroline was out of breath from speaking so quickly. But she looked happy and excited.

The class had been listening quietly to every word Caroline said. No one said anything for a moment. Everyone looked at Angelina with admiration. It was as though Angelina were a real pioneer from history. Jessica thought Angelina was the most interesting and beautiful doll in the world.

"I think that's fascinating," Mrs. Otis finally said. "And, you know, Caroline. It looks like you have more than just a doll collection."

"What do you mean?" Caroline asked.

"You have a collection of relatives who all had Angelina when they were girls," the teacher said. "And you have a collection of countries and states where Angelina has lived and traveled. You have a collection of stickers to prove it."

"That's true," Caroline said, looking prouder than ever.

"What about the rest of your porcelain dolls?" Lila called out. "Did they travel across America, too?"

Caroline looked at the floor. "Well . . ."

"Are they all as beautiful as Angelina?" Eva asked.

"Yes, tell us about your other dolls," Jessica begged.

Jessica heard Elizabeth take a deep breath. She looked at her sister. Elizabeth was staring straight at Caroline, and she looked nervous. Jessica wondered why.

"How many dolls *do* you have, Caroline?" Mrs. Otis asked.

CHAPTER 9

The Truth

Elizabeth held her breath. She knew Caroline had to tell the truth. But she also knew that it would be difficult for Caroline to admit to everyone she had been lying.

Caroline held Angelina close and looked sadly at Elizabeth. The room was silent.

"Caroline?" Mrs. Otis asked, sounding puzzled. "How many dolls are in your collection?"

"Just one," Caroline whispered. "Just Angelina."

"What?" Lila said loudly. "You said you had a whole bunch!"

"I know, but—" Caroline looked like she was going to cry.

Elizabeth felt happy that Caroline had had the courage to tell the truth. She also felt sorry for Caroline because now the kids would tease her even more.

"You were bragging and bragging," Jessica said angrily. "You were just making it up. I knew it all the time!"

Elizabeth nudged Jessica with her elbow. "Stop it," she whispered. Jessica pretended that she didn't hear her.

"You certainly were exaggerating, Caroline," Mrs. Otis said sternly. "But I'm so glad you told the truth. Angelina is a wonderful doll all by herself. I know you must be very proud of her. And you should all remember that every collection has to start with one item."

"She could get more," Elizabeth spoke up. She smiled at Caroline. "Right?"

Caroline nodded. "I am going to, someday!" she said. "I even have a magazine all about porcelain doll collecting."

She ran to her desk where Angelina's case was and took out a wrinkled magazine. Elizabeth could see it was full of pictures and descriptions of dolls.

"I'm getting this one next," Caroline said. "When I save enough birthday money." She held it up for everyone to see.

Jessica leaned forward in her chair. "I can't see it," she said.

Lila was trying to see the picture, too, but she was also trying to act as though she didn't care.

Elizabeth stood up and walked over to Caroline. "Can I see it?" she asked.

The picture showed a porcelain doll with blond hair and blue-green eyes—just like Elizabeth. Elizabeth couldn't help smiling. "She looks like me and Jessica," she said.

"Let me see!" Jessica said, jumping up.

One by one, the other girls stood up to look at the doll magazine. Caroline pointed out several dolls. Elizabeth was impressed by how much Caroline knew about each one.

"And when I have a daughter, I'll give Angelina to her," Caroline said proudly.

"And all the rest of your dolls, too," Elizabeth said. "When you get them."

Caroline smiled. "That's right," she said.

"OK, everyone," Mrs. Otis said. "Let's get back to our seats. We'll show the rest of the collections at the end of the day. And you two," she added, pointing to Charlie and Jerry, "will stay in during recess so we can have a talk about what you did."

Jessica looked at Elizabeth and said, "I told you they'd get in trouble."

Elizabeth smiled. The most important thing was that Caroline had Angelina back, and that she had admitted the truth.

CHAPTER 10

Lila's Fabulous Collection

Jessica was nervous about showing her "Jessica" collection. Elizabeth had promised that it was a good idea, but Jessica wasn't completely sure.

At last, there were only two collections left to see: Jessica's and Lila's. Lila raised her hand.

"Can I go now?" she asked Mrs. Otis. "I don't want to go last."

Mrs. Otis looked at Jessica. "Is that OK with you?"

"I don't care," Jessica answered. She pulled

her shopping bag full of "Jessica" things closer to her and smiled at Lila. "You first."

Lila stood up. "This is what I brought," she announced, taking a pretty pink purse to the front of the room. She opened it up and out spilled a tangle of hair ribbons, barrettes, and bows.

"My father bought me this one in New York City," Lila said, holding up a large clip-on blue bow. "And this is one I bought with my own money at Disneyland."

Jessica was surprised. Lila's collection wasn't so wonderful at all. Elizabeth poked her in the side, and Jessica turned.

"Aren't you glad you didn't bring your hair things?" Elizabeth asked with a giggle.

"I sure am," Jessica whispered back, smiling.

"Who cares about ribbons and stuff like that?" Ken said to Todd.

"I think those are very nice, Lila," Mrs. Otis said. "All collections are special because they tell us something about the person whose collection it is."

"What does that tell us about Lila?" Winston Egbert asked. "That she looks in the mirror all the time?"

Some of the kids began to laugh. Jessica couldn't help smiling. Then she raised her hand.

"Is it my turn now?" Jessica asked Mrs. Otis.

"Go ahead, Jessica," Mrs. Otis said.

Taking a deep breath, Jessica walked to the front of the classroom and emptied her shopping bag. "I brought in everything I have that has my name on it," she explained. "Because we're twins, a lot of people think

Elizabeth and I are the same. So it's important to let people know I'm Jessica."

One by one, she held up her toothbrush, license plate, sweatshirt, T-shirt, shoelaces—the whole "Jessica collection." Everyone was surprised at how many things she owned with her name printed on it.

"I think you have a very good explanation for your collection," Mrs. Otis said. "Twins have to work extra hard to be individuals."

"But it's still the best thing in the world to have a twin sister," Jessica said quickly. She gave Elizabeth a big smile.

Elizabeth smiled back. Collection day had turned out well for everyone.

Jessica and Elizabeth were in their room after school. Elizabeth put down her book and sniffed the air.

"What's that awful smell?" she asked.

Jessica held her nose. "It's coming from Steven's room. I hope he's almost finished with his science project," she said.

"Well, you won't have to wait any longer," Steven said, coming into his sisters' room. "I'm taking my project to school tomorrow. It came out great."

"Can we see it?" Elizabeth asked. She got up from the floor and headed for the doorway.

Steven put his hand out to stop her. "I'll show it to you but you have to listen to my presentation, too. I know you'll think it's great," he said.

Jessica looked at Elizabeth. They shrugged their shoulders. "OK," Jessica said, "but don't take too long."

The twins followed their older brother into his room. On his desk was a miniature volcano

that erupted and then created a wave in a pan of water. Elizabeth and Jessica listened as Steven read through his presentation.

"It's boring, Steven," Jessica said. "Everyone will fall asleep by the time you're done."

"Well, I'll bet I win first prize for my grade," Steven said firmly. "Then you'll be sorry you laughed."

"Why don't we make a real bet," Jessica said. "If you win, we'll do all your chores for a week. If you lose, you'll have to do everything for us."

"That's a great idea," Elizabeth said. "But you have to win *first* prize," she told Steven.

Steven smiled. "Just wait and see. I'll win, and then you'll have to do everything I say!"

Who will win the bet? Find out in Sweet Valley Kids #18, BOSSY STEVEN.

(SVK Super Snooper #2)

920742